Shirley 4 President
by LaShon Ormond

Illustration and Design
by Frank Lunar & Ashe Ah-Sing

Copyright:
All Content and Images ©2018
All rights reserved.
Real GIRLS Enterprises

ISBN: 978-1986570572

LASHON ORMOND'S SHIRLEY 4 PRESIDENT

To all of the girls who continue to be the firsts: don't
ever let fear make you give up on your dreams!

And to my sister-friend, Kercena: Keep being a
voice for those whose cries often go unheard.

This world needs you!

My name is Shirley and I am running for president. The boys in my class say a girl could never be president because, well because, she's not a boy. And that's not true! My Grandma Emily, who lives in Barbados, says girls can do just about anything boys can do and some things they can't.

Come to think of it, she also tells me that my mouth is going to get me in trouble but I'm just going to think about her advice about girls for now because I agree with her.

So, like I said, I am running for president. I know you may be thinking where could I have possibly gotten such a crazy idea. Well, it's not that crazy. Two nights ago, I had a dream that I was running for President of the United States. In my dream, people were saying that I was crazy.

One reporter even asked me if I knew I was a Black woman. And he said no woman could ever be president. Some questions don't deserve an answer. And so I did not respond to him. "Next," I said to the reporter standing behind him.

Anyway, there I was, in this dream, giving interviews and speeches, explaining why a woman would make a good, no, make that a great president. I had campaign hats and buttons that said "Unbought and Unbossed". I probably should have added "and Unbothered" because clearly I was unbothered by the ridiculous questions that people asked me about my decision to run.

It is kind of funny that this was my campaign slogan because my family and my friends are always telling me how bossy I am. And my parents are always, always, always telling me to stop bossing my sisters around.

I don't think I'm being bossy; I'm just giving out instructions about the best way to do stuff.

Even Mrs. Smith, who lives in my neighborhood and teaches at my school, calls me
Miss Bossy Pants.

But in my dream, they were not calling me Miss Bossy Pants, they were calling me Congresswoman.

Yesterday, I told my best friend, Pamela, about my dream and she just shook her head. Today, my teacher announced that we are having class elections. For me, that is a sign that I should run for and become president. Pamela does not think I can beat Bobby in the election.

She said he's so cute that all of the girls will vote for him and so cool that all the boys will vote for him. Besides, he's already handing out treats and putting up posters.

But that's okay; I will get started today. I don't have money to buy everyone treats but I know the things that my classmates want and I know how to convince the grownups to give them to us.

The rest will take care of itself.

And since someday I am going to be Congresswoman Shirley and someday I will run for the President of these United States, I need to start practicing so I can be prepared for that amazing day.

In order to run for class president, I have to complete the application and meet all of the requirements. Only then can I announce my candidacy. It sounds like a lot but I will do whatever it takes.

Yes, I meet all of the requirements. I'm a student at PS 84 and I'm in a sixth grade homeroom now, after a small stint in a third grade room.

Okay, long crazy story that I will make short - I started school early in Barbados but they didn't teach us any American history there so they demoted me two grades when I came back to Brooklyn until they realized how smart I was and that I could catch up on the American history without being in a class with third graders - WHEW!!!!

I make all A's so no, I haven't failed any classes.

Mrs. Smith approved my application. She said she was impressed and once again reminded me that I was the first girl to run for class president. I said, well, I think that's sad but someone has to go first so it might as well be me.

I hope more girls will run after I win. She laughed and said she hopes so, too, calling me Madam President Sassy Pants.

You know, I think grownups have a hard time finding the right words for smart, outspoken, confident girls who can be leaders. When I'm an adult, I will make sure that I use the right words to describe the intelligent little girls I encounter.

My friend, Frank, is an excellent artist and since I'm always helping him with math, he agreed to help make some posters.

And since Pam wants to hang out with me while Frank is making posters (because she has a crush on him), she agreed to listen to my speech and give me some feedback...

...even though she still says I'm crazy.

Mark wants to be a journalist so he is going to be the reporter that asks me the really hard questions during the debate. I tell my sisters they have to sit in the audience and listen to my speech.

And my Dad, well, he's just going to sit in the living room and be my Dad because boys are coming over to our house.

On election day, there will be an assembly in the auditorium and we have to give our speeches in front of the whole sixth grade and Principal Erwin so I have to practice.

I cannot be nervous. Bobby talks to people all of the time so I know he will do well.

After two weeks of making and hanging up posters and practicing my speech AND explaining why a girl wants to be class president, Election Day has arrived. The auditorium wall has everyone's posters on display. Some of our classmates are holding up signs.

Mrs. Smith says this is allowed as long as they're respectful. I spot one that says Shirley for President. Another one says May The Best Girl Win. I smile at that one. There's only one girl in the race and that's me!

Principal Erwin calls everyone to attention.

He reminds us of the importance of respecting each speaker and the consequences for not doing so. Then Mrs. Harris comes to the podium. She's holding a basket with all of the candidates' names in it. She pulls them out, one at a time.

Bobby
Michael
Eric
Shirley

I cannot believe it. Mine is the last name pulled out of the basket. I roll my eyes.

Humph - Whatever happened to ladies first?

Bobby goes first. He reminds us of all of the great treats he's given out and promises that there will be more if he is president.

Somehow, I don't believe this is true. Principal Erwin doesn't like us kids getting all filled up on junk food unless it is a special day.

Michael stands on stage next. He talks a lot about the need for better science lab stuff.

That's Michael. He is going to be a great scientist so he wants our school to get better equipment so he can practice.

Eric talks about better uniforms for the basketball team, new jerseys for the football team and prettier cheerleaders.

In my mind, I think he's a jerk for saying that but the rules say we have to be respectful of all speakers (I guess that means even when they're not being respectful of the audience).

Besides, I can't focus on that because now it's my turn.

Some of the girls stand up and clap before I begin my speech. My Dad would call that solidarity and so would Mr. Webster...as in Webster's dictionary. Yeah, when we get in trouble my mother makes us write words from the dictionary. The other day I called my sister stupid and Mom said I should find other S words to use. So that I would have some in my vocabulary, she decided that I should spend ALL DAY Saturday copying some of them while my sisters went to the movies - SIGH. SO SAD.

She said, "Let's see how many other words you could have used." There are a lot of them. S must be the most popular letter in the alphabet or it sure felt that way on Saturday.

Anyway, Principal Erwin looks at the girls sternly and they all take their seats. Then I begin. I talk about the importance of breakfast and lunch for all students because so many parents are not able to provide food for their kids. I say I want us to beautify our school. I talk about other important stuff like the science lab, uniforms and better books in the library.

I give a really good speech and I think I have a good chance of winning.

Principal Erwin comes back to the podium and reads the rules. Each person has one vote. Everyone in the sixth grade can vote for sixth grade class president. There can only be one winner. If there is a tie, we will have to vote to break the tie.

Each person will be given one ballot with our four names on it. Circle only one name. If you circle more than one name, your vote does not count. The winner will be announced tomorrow. We make our choices and drop our ballots in the boxes at the door and we go back to back to class.

At recess, some girls said they couldn't vote for me because girls shouldn't be president. Others say Bobby was so cute they had to vote for him.

The Solidarity Girls say they voted for me.

And the boys, well the boys voted for the boys.

In the end, Bobby gets the most votes.

Today, I am asking Mr. Edwards to donate paint so that we can make our school better. Every month, I will write a letter to my Congressman asking for money for better books in our library and better science equipment.

And every week, I will visit our Assemblyman's office to see if there was a way for everyone to get breakfast and lunch.

This is what I planned to do as Class President. I will still do it.

I am not class president but I am a citizen of my school community. I am not class president but I am a leader. I am not class president but I am determined to make a difference.

Mr. Edwards says I am a little rebel. I say yes, I rebel against the limitations others try to set for me.

Everyone should be a rebel...

Shirley 4 President! was inspired by Shirley Anita St. Hill Chisholm. Mrs. Chisholm was born in Brooklyn, New York on November 30, 1924. She was the oldest of four girls raised by her parents, Charles St. Hill, a factory worker from Guyana and Ruby Seale St. Hill, a seamstress from Barbados. When the Great Depression hit America, Shirley and her sister were sent to live with their grandparents on their farm in Barbados while her parents worked on building a place to settle their family in Bedford-Stuyvestant.

Mrs. Chisholm was a politician, an educator and an activist. She was the first Black woman in America elected to the United States Congress in 1968. She was very outspoken and not a very traditional member of Congress. Some referred to her as "Fighting Shirley" but she simply believed it was her duty to represent the people.

Congresswoman Chisholm used her influence to work for the causes she raised in her campaign. In 1972, Congresswoman Chisholm decided to run for the Democratic nomination for President of the United States and though she did not win, she was able to get her name on ballots in 12 districts and received 10% of the delegate votes at the National Democratic Convention.

Throughout her life, Congresswoman Chisholm continued to be a great leader, whose goal was not to gain favor with influential politicians but to be a difference maker for those whose lives were strained because of great poverty, discriminatory practices, and unfair and unjust laws. Congresswoman Chisholm was a pioneer but more than that she was a warrior for the people.

Mrs. Chisholm died on January 1, 2005 in Ormond Beach, Florida.

Made in the USA
San Bernardino, CA
25 January 2020